"But why are you out here?" Mary said. "Where did you come from?"

"Been sleeping in them pines. Got nowhere else I can go."

"Let's try again. Why are you in this dream? In this tent? I have no idea who you are."

The girl finally drew back enough for Mary to see her face. Her wide eyes were solid black in the flashlight's beam.

"Ain't been nothing warm out here for long as I can remember. Can't remember my name either. Been lookin' for my husband so long, never spoke to a living soul until you."

She froze, staring over Mary's shoulder, trembling harder by the second. She put her head down and wrapped her arms around Mary, squeezing tight.

"Train coming," the girl said, her voice urgent but getting lower and softer. "Longest train you ever saw. Devil driving that train, took my husband away with him. Been trying hard to take me but I hide."

Mary opened her mouth to ask what she was really hiding from when she heard a strange, ringing noise, gradually rising until it was louder than the wind.

She'd heard that metallic hum many times, but she couldn't possibly be hearing it on this mountain.

The singing of the rails, the distant sound of a fast train getting closer.

To my grandfather, Fred Steffey

A long-working railroad man,
Quick with a laugh and a smile,
Even quicker with a tall tale.

IN THE PINES

KARI KILGORE

SPIRAL PUBLISHING, LTD.

Chapter 1

2015

Mary Robbins stretched her legs out, groaning at the warmth of the fire against her aching feet and muscles. The ancient oak, maple, and locust trees soaring overhead sported dark green leaves poking through the bright springtime shades, but a distinct chill lingered in the North Georgia early evening air.

The view across the granite and limestone gorge opened up barely twenty yards away, the river at the bottom hundreds of feet below as musical as it was beautiful. A skeletal frame of bright new wood suggested what the observation deck would look like in a couple of weeks. The gorgeous scenery would draw people to the grand opening, and the bike trail she was helping build would bring them back.

The antiquated narrow-gauge rails were long since removed, probably hauled off for scrap decades before, saving the crew gathered around the fire the work of pulling them up now. A stack of decaying cross ties waited beside the emerging bike trail for the four-wheelers and bigger ATVs to carry away.

Those same noisy, stinky vehicles would be banned from this trail once it opened, but Mary and everyone else working on the trail was glad they were here for this phase.

The road and parking lot less than a mile away weren't passable yet, and no one wanted to pack in the heavy equipment, food, or camping gear miles on foot or on a bicycle. Opening day in June would be soon enough to tackle this steep climb without any fossil fuel assistance.

Mary held her hands out to the heat of the fire, her pale palms contrasting with her much darker hands and arms, then brushed her fingers over the cargo pocket on her thigh.

The strange watch she'd found was still there.

She'd noticed the glint of the gold case beside one of the tracks the ATVs had churned in the red clay right before the crew knocked off for the night. She was almost certain it was an antique railroad watch. Even in a coating of that heavy soil, it looked remarkably like one her great-uncle carried.

She wasn't sure why she'd slipped it into her pocket instead of turning it in for the museum in the ghost of a town at the bottom of the mountain. She planned to do just that. Eventually. A strange catch in her mind, and in her heart, begged her to hold onto it just a little bit longer.

As if anyone around her could read her vaguely guilty thoughts, Mary jumped when an empty water bottle bounced off her thigh. Lisa Dewey, the crew leader, grinned at Mary.

"Still with us, Ms. Robbins? We can help you get your tent set up if you're ready to crash."

"Not just yet," Mary said, unable to hide a yawn. "I'm not about to be first to bed in this bunch."

Fifteen people, half men, half women, were getting this

trail through the North Georgia mountains cleaned up and ready to go. Mary had taken several of these working vacations with the three women sitting closest to her, and with her wife, but she hadn't been out on a trail for a little over two years now.

Not since Rachel died.

Long absence from such hard work had her feeling the strain, but this was also her first bike trail. With a cleared railway there wasn't much digging through roots or struggling with boulders as on a brand new forest path, but shoveling endless loads of huge ballast gravel, then increasingly smaller layers over top of it had her back, hands, and shoulders aching. Tomorrow they'd shift to building several raised platforms for camping and a restroom facility before moving to the next trail section.

"Don't worry about it, Mar," her friend Mia Chen said, pulling the clip out of her long, shining black hair. "I'll go first, as usual."

"Looks to me like the rest of us aren't far behind," Lisa said. "Bike trails are a bit tougher than most people expect. I'll let you all sleep in before we turn into carpenters. Breakfast at eight, then we're back at it."

Mary let Mia pretend to help her up, though she certainly would have overbalanced her dainty friend. Mia stood not quite as high as Mary's shoulder.

"I'm even more jealous of your new 'do after today," Mia said. "This mop on my head is burning me up, but Josh whines when I cut it."

Mary touched her dark brown hair, the barely quarter inch of curls tight and strangely thick under her fingers. She hadn't gotten used to that change yet, but it was far cooler.

"Yeah, Rachel liked mine longer, too."

"Oh hell, I'm sorry." Mia closed her eyes and turning her

head away. "I'm too weary to keep track of my mouth. Need help with your setup?"

Mary knew her friend was just worried about her, but the taboo subjects and anxious glances her way were getting on her nerves. If Mia was convinced Mary wasn't ready for this, why had she badgered and pushed for the trip in the first place?

"Nah, I'm good." Mary waved toward the far end of the clearing. "I think I'm heading out to those pines over there. We drove up to Michigan to camp all the time when I was a kid. The breeze sounds amazing through them at night. I always slept like a baby."

Mia's dark brown eyes widened, but she couldn't quite hide her smile. She'd been on almost all of these trail building trips with Mary and Rachel over the past several years. Fear didn't seem to be a part of her reality, much less her vocabulary.

"Right next to the woods? Good luck with that."

Mary didn't think twice about setting up far away from the rest of the group, not anymore. She'd started having awful nightmares when the car crash took Rachel. They were different from night to night, but it was generally variations on a theme. What Mary could have done to stop it, or at least stop it enough to still have Rachel. Who, or what, she could have bargained with to make it turn out any other way.

She knew her dreams would keep anyone sleeping near her awake all night.

The mesh skylight in her cozy tent made for fantastic star watching, though she wouldn't see much under the trees tonight. The lullaby whisper of the pines would be worth it. The clear ground and lack of undergrowth made for quick work setting up her tent.

She was crawling inside her sleeping bag with a sigh

before anyone closer to the fire was finished, in bed first after all. She tucked the muddy watch under her backpack.

"'Night, sweetheart," Mary whispered, same as she had every night without Rachel. That was the only thing that let her get to sleep at all. "Love you."

Mary barely managed to turn over and pull her sleeping bag up to her ears before she was out.

Chapter 2

CHATTERING teeth woke Mary a few hours later, and at first she thought they were her own.

She was certainly cold enough for that. The temperature in the tent had to be a lot lower than the fifties she and everyone else had prepared for. The air felt frozen in her nose and lungs. She started to pull one arm out of her bag to reach for her jacket, then stopped.

Someone, or something, was in the tent, pushed hard against her chest and belly. The chattering was coming from her unknown bed guest. Mary blinked, trying to get her bearings. She couldn't imagine some kind of animal unzipping her tent door and getting inside, but no one in the camp would do that, either.

This wasn't the strangest dream she'd ever had, but it might be close. More than one therapist had told her to engage with her nightmares, try to figure out what her subconscious was telling her. No time like the present.

"Who's there?" she whispered, her own shivering making her voice tremble.

The body twitched but didn't move away. Surely any

animal would take off when she spoke, unless it was some kind of sentient dream creature. Wouldn't be the first one Mary had met. She moved her arm slowly out from under her pillow, reaching for her flashlight.

"Listen, I'm not going to hurt you if you don't hurt me," she said, keeping her voice low. "Where did you come from?"

Her fingers, numb from the cold, found the metal body of her light. It felt warm to her for some reason, as if it had been outside by the fire. She usually couldn't operate electronic things in a dream, but something this simple should work. Mary pushed the button, squinting against the glaring bright light.

A girl's voice moaned, and Mary felt arms wrap around her waist. She blinked several times, but every time she kept seeing a snarl of kinky black hair and nothing else. She tried to move back to get a better look, but the girl only moved with her. As her vision cleared, she saw bare arms as dark brown as her own, rippling with gooseflesh.

"Okay. You can see I don't have a gun or a club, and I can see you're not Bigfoot trying to get me into the sack," Mary said, trying to calm herself as much as the girl. "Let me figure out what's going on here. What's your name? Why are you in my dream?"

"That wind so cold." The girl spoke in a slow, singsong accent, not moving away from Mary. "So cold."

The tent shuddered, the wires anchoring it to the ground thrumming in the frigid gust. Mary tried to make a mental note to ask Mia what the deal was with this crazy weather that intruded into a dream. Her notes didn't always survive waking up in the morning.

"But why are you out here?" Mary said. "Where did you come from?"

"Been sleeping in them pines. Got nowhere else I can go."

"Let's try again. Why are you in this dream? In this tent? I have no idea who you are."

The girl finally drew back enough for Mary to see her face. She wasn't quite as young as Mary thought, maybe twenty years old but as small as a child. Her wide eyes looked solid black in the flashlight's beam.

"Ain't been nothing warm out here for long as I can remember. Can't remember my name either. Been lookin' for my husband so long, never spoke to a living soul until you. Railroad man, name of…"

She froze, staring over Mary's shoulder, trembling harder by the second. Mary had just about decided it was worth the risk to turn and see what kind of monster her sleep-addled brain had come up with when the girl moaned again. She put her head down and wrapped her arms around Mary, squeezing tight.

"Train coming," the girl said, her voice urgent but getting lower and softer. "Longest train you ever saw. Devil driving that train, took my husband away with him. Been trying hard to take me but I hide."

Mary opened her mouth to ask what she was really hiding from when she heard a strange, ringing noise, gradually rising until it was louder than the wind. She'd heard that metallic hum many times, but she couldn't possibly be hearing it on this mountain.

The singing of the rails, the distant sound of a fast train getting closer.

"There's no train." Mary pulled her jacket over the girl's painfully thin shoulders and arms. Her eyes had adjusted well enough to see the girl only wore a dirty cotton shift, stained brown and green. "Those tracks are long gone, I promise. The last train ran decades ago."

"Where that sound come from then?" The girl's whisper was high pitched and breathy, making her sound like the terrified child she appeared to be. "And that awful cold wind?"

The tent shuddered, and Mary felt the bottom lift off the ground enough for the frigid air to pass underneath. She couldn't imagine how the anchors could hold much longer, unless they were made of steel cables in this dream world.

The eerie notes of the rails were drowned out by the screech of metal as the train got closer, then the noise rose to ear-splitting levels when the brakes engaged. The girl squeezed hard enough to take Mary's breath, and her shriek was louder than the train's.

The sharp hiss of steam right outside the tent walls brought a scream to Mary's throat at last.

Chapter 3

1985

George Evans held one of his boyhood books, pretending to read. He ran his fingertips over the rough cloth cover of *Treasure Island*, watching his grandfather stare at the television. Decades of squinting and suntans marked Adam Evans's pale face with deep lines, the thick light brown hair of his youth reduced to a delicate gray cloud around the back of his skull.

A cable channel with endless black-and-white reruns clashed with the brand new television. Even with a twenty-seven inch screen, it was the first in this house that wasn't big enough to serve as furniture.

The last early Seventies model had faded to all pastel colors and the picture rolled constantly, but the eldest Evans still complained about the modern version fairly often. He claimed to despise the plastic wood grain when he'd had a real wooden set before. The new television was rarely ever turned off, though.

George imagined thousands of people in his and even his

father's generation, millions maybe. All struck by that same odd combination of never-ending reruns and parental disappointment but clueless what to do about it.

The bedroom was too hot, like always, and the smell of old man flesh was stronger than he remembered from just a few months ago. Every shelf and surface around the low hospital-style bed was jammed full of stuff. More old books, pictures, and what George could only call junk. But of course his grandfather would liven right up and pitch a conniption fit if anyone so much as moved a single thing, much less tried to thin some of it out.

Adam Evans never missed much, even as he seemed to recede into the past.

The door was open just a crack, enough so George could hear his daughter Sandy in the living room. She'd been wandering around the rest of the house for the past two days, lugging her expensive Betamax recorder on her shoulder and narrating like she was on an archaeological dig. He supposed at fifteen and growing up a Chicago girl, that was exactly how she felt.

George had vowed to himself not to say a word about how many recording tapes she went through as long as she paid for them. He hadn't even fought all that hard about her determined choice of smaller, pricier Betamax over VHS once she made his head spin with technical explanations about better recording quality.

This long vacation in Georgia was already testing his vow to keep his mouth shut about the constant recording and expense.

Sandy was naturally a whole lot more interested in her friends than her parents, probably would be for a few years to come. He'd been the same way at fifteen, just without a video camera on his shoulder constantly making recordings for an advanced audio/visual class. George's plan of getting the kid to spend time with her great-grandfather while his own parents were on vacation was working about as well as most of his big ideas had lately.

Well, he could do something about this one whether anyone else in the tiny, crowded house approved or not.

"Where you going, Grandbaby?" his grandfather said, not making any move to get out of his power lift recliner or taking his eyes from the TV screen.

"I think it's about time Sandy took a break and spent some time with us." George stretched, then picked up his and the old man's empty glasses. "Want some more water, Grandad?"

"I reckon, only if you're getting some for yourself. Don't bother that girl, now. She's like to be bored to tears by an old fart like me."

"Well, she's bored by an old fart like me, too," George said from the doorway. "Doesn't mean she can't come in here and make an effort. Maybe you can tell her a story."

Adam snorted and shook his head, and George forced himself not to do the same. He gritted his teeth instead, making sure he put on at least a neutral face before he talked to Sandy. The kid was way too damn smart to fall for fake family togetherness, no matter how hard George tried to create it out of thin air. She'd just have to make do.

Sandy didn't bother to look up when an oak floorboard creaked under George's feet. She was sprawled across the ancient velvet couch, her multi-colored canvas sneakers up on the faded flower print his grandmother had been so proud of.

George tried his best to keep his opinions of his daughter's sky-high teased reddish-brown bangs and silly side ponytail to himself. His grandmother would not have kept her mouth shut, and his mother had her say once in a while.

Both women would have had a field day with Sandy's garish green and purple plaid shirt and black stirrup pants, too.

She had the video camera plugged into the wall, staring at the tiny display with exactly the same vacant expression as the man over eighty years her senior in the other room.

George forced himself to smile.

"Hey Sandy. Think it's time you came in and spent some time with your great-grandfather?"

"Hey Dad. Nah, I'm busy right now. Maybe later, okay?"

"No, not okay. You've been in here for hours. Come on, help me in the kitchen. Feet off the couch, too."

Sandy rolled her eyes and sighed, a common enough reaction that George didn't even respond anymore. She wasn't sighing at him, exactly. More at the never-ending indignation of being fifteen years old and knowing better than everyone around her. He might wish he could save her from acting that way, but he knew from his own childhood that only growing up would do that for her.

At least she stomped her feet on the floor instead of continuing to ignore him.

"Dad," she whispered, glancing toward the old man's bedroom as she stood beside him. "I don't know what to talk to him about. Greatgrand kind of scares me."

George bit his cheeks to keep from smiling. How many times did he feel that way with his own daughter and her friends?

"Well, he's probably scared of you, hon. He raised three rowdy boys, remember? Not a girl in sight till my dad was nearly grown."

She followed him into the kitchen, grabbing a Coke from the ancient, rumbly green refrigerator. George managed not to say anything about the sugar as he filled two glasses with water. His own mouth was watering for the sharp bite and sweet coolness of a Coca-Cola right now, but he didn't want to tempt his grandfather.

"Finish that in here, Sandy. Greatgrand can't have them."

"Fine." She downed half of it in one gulp. "What am I supposed to do, just sit there watching him stare at that lame old junk on TV?"

"Nope, that's what I've been doing. We talked about everything years ago, I think, same with my dad. Time for you two to get to know each other while you still can. Listen, you've been wandering around recording videos since we got here. Why don't you interview him?"

Sandy scowled, the corners of her mouth pulling in to match her eyebrows, looking so much like her mother that George's smile finally broke through. He missed his wife, stuck at a business convention back in Chicago, more than he wanted to admit. With the massive, overcrowded conference center and nowhere near enough pay phones, they usually didn't even talk until Bev got home late at night.

"Interview him? Jeez, Dad, great idea. What exactly should I interview him about? How great the Sixties really were?"

"Well, kid, that would be interviewing me, believe it or not. Ask him about the stuff around the house. Didn't you say you like some of it?"

Sandy finished her soda, crumpling up the can before dropping it into the garbage. She caught her goofy ponytail in one hand, twisting the end between her fingers.

"I guess so. Maybe. I could take pictures and put the video with it, I suppose. We're gonna learn editing in the fall."

"Now you're talking." George picked up the glasses of water and his grandfather's latest dose of pills, already sorted into white cups, off the spotless baby blue tiled countertop. His father and mother were right. The visiting nurses and housekeeper were worth every penny. "He has a lot of stories to tell. Just hasn't had anyone to tell them to in a long time. Grab those saltines, will you? He needs something with his medicine."

She sighed again, but with her back to him George couldn't tell if she rolled her eyes or not.

He decided on not. Someone had to be the optimist stuck in the house with these two for another week.

Chapter 4

THE OLDER MAN hadn't moved when George walked into the room, but his lined face lit up when he saw Sandy. About thirty years fell away in that instant.

"Sandy girl! Come in here to keep your old great-granddad company for a little while?"

"Hey Greatgrand," Sandy said, leaning down to hug him. "Thought you'd like someone more interesting than Dad here."

"Ain't that the truth." Adam swallowed the pills in one practiced gulp, then took a handful of the crackers Sandy held out for him. "You give us both something to smile about."

George settled back into his faded and worn recliner, a far less fancy edition than his grandfather's power chair. Both had been dragged in here from the living room a few years ago when the majority of the Adam Evans Maintenance Operation compressed into the much smaller space. That same reduction of the old man's movements explained why every available spot was crammed full of Adam's memories, much of it rescued from elsewhere in the house.

Sandy wandered around the room, running her fingers along the knick-knacks and mementos crowded onto the shelves. He'd seen her do that before in their house in Chicago and in his parents' house before she made one of those videos for her class or for herself.

She hadn't found her focus yet, but she would.

"What's this, Greatgrand?" She stepped closer to a small frame, nearly hidden among all the photos on the wall.

"Can't see from here, hon. Grab it down and reach it to me."

Sandy lifted the frame from the wall and held it carefully, waiting for him to take it. George stared at their hands, fascinated and saddened by his grandfather's wrinkled, spotted flesh compared to his daughter's smooth, pale skin.

"This here's scrip. It's how we got paid, Sandy," Adam said. The frame held several pieces of paper, faded and worn. Coins lined the edges, all different sizes with oddly shaped holes punched right through the metal. "They didn't give us money we could spend just anywhere. Had to give it right back to 'em at their own stores!"

"Did you ever get paid that way, Dad?" Sandy said, one eyebrow raised.

He was sure she was teasing him. Mostly sure.

"Not quite. I missed that era by a year or two, I guess. Where'd you get that, Granddad?"

"Oh, bunch of old boys I worked with rounded it up when I retired." He squinted at the paper, then carefully propped the frame up on the table beside his chair. "I was the only one left who remembered it, least here in Atlanta. Might be some up there in Chicago where y'all live."

Sandy tapped her bright blue fingernail on a framed document. George recognized his great-grandparents' wedding certificate and smiled. The paper was thin and yellowing, the print surprisingly plain and businesslike.

"State of Georgia, County of DeKalb," Sandy said, twisting her flat Chicago accent into a passable Southern. She even got the county right instead of mixing it up with the Illinois town, though she laid it on a bit thick with the DeCaaaab. "Adam Evenschmidt and Ms. Delia Andrews. When did you change your name, Greatgrand?"

"Not 'til after the first World War started," he said. "You see right below there, my Army walking papers?"

"Honorable Discharge from the United States Army," Sandy said in her normal accent. "Yep, right there. Adam Evans, 1918."

"I wasn't real happy about that," he said, his mouth turning down. "Easiest thing for all of us at the time, though. Been Evans so long I hardly remember starting out with a different name. Feels like that life was nothing but a ghost sometimes."

"Sandy loves ghost stories, Granddad," George said. "She's always reading them or watching movies about them. I bet she's never heard about the ghost train."

Sandy's blue eyes lit up, just like her great-grandfather's had when she walked in. She settled down on the ottoman in front of him. The huge footstool was far older than she was, still covered with the same strange flat flowery velvet as the living room set.

George's chest warmed and his eyes got a little bit hot, watching his grandfather and his daughter finally connect.

"Ghost train?" she said. "Here?"

"Naah, not here in the city, not as I know of. This one's way up in the mountains, almost in North Carolina. Town called Gossdale."

He took a drink of water and leaned back, ready to get into his tale. The beverage of choice may have gotten a lot less potent since George was a little boy, but the ritual hadn't.

"Got your camera, Sandy?" he said under his breath, trying not to roll his own eyes.

She drew back and shook her head, then jumped up and darted out of the room. Just as George wondered if she'd made a break for it, she rushed back in with the camera and a tripod almost as tall as she was. Before either man could blink, she had the whole thing set up and focused.

"Don't worry about this, Greatgrand," she said, sitting back down, kicking her shoes off, and crossing her feet under her knees. "Just pretend it's not there."

"Well, since I don't know what the heck it is, I'll sure do just that."

He leaned his head back and closed his eyes. Sandy stared at George, silently asking why he'd dragged her in here if the old man was just going to fall asleep. He winked and shook his head.

All part of the ritual.

When Adam Evans opened his eyes a few seconds later, he seemed like a middle-aged man reminiscing with his drinking buddies, not a grizzled railroad retiree approaching one hundred years old.

Chapter 5

"Course I can tell you about that ghost train," Adam Evans said, nodding. "Whole thing happened right in front of my own eyes. Yeah, I started work on that train long time ago, when I was not quite the age you are right now. Had too many people to feed and not enough work to feed 'em, so that was the end of schooling for me."

He said work in an old way, almost like wo-eek. George and Sandy were watching him go back in time, his accent shifting from musical old Georgia to that poor, uneducated teenager he'd been. Neither George nor his father had ever been sure how much was playing up for his audience and how much was distant reality.

"Good men on that train, good to me and all them other boys. Least till we got a new conductor. Captain." Adam snorted and shook his head. "Insisted we call him that, never mind what we called every other conductor we ever had. Came out the Confederate Army, ran those trains during the War. Thought that old Southern way was the only way to be.

"Course how I heard it told, his rich daddy bought him that command, mainly cause all he knew how to do was make trouble for his family. Imagine they was like a lot of families back then, lost it all during the War. More men than you know traded on that faded old uniform back then. No money, no land, no skills, no other way to live.

"This was a private line, now, no rules and regulations like I had the rest of my working years, not like your daddy does now, or even like his daddy did. Owners of that line, they did what they wanted to back in them days. Seemed to think hiring that Captain for show would draw people in just so they could watch him parade up and down like a raggedy banty rooster. That was about all he was good for, but he never grasped onto that for himself."

Adam stared at the frame full of scrip beside him, his eyes soft and unfocused. Despite that, George knew his mind was more present than it had been in weeks.

"One of the good men we had, one of the best, was J.W. Gartin. Came up out of south Georgia. Had a pretty little wife, just a whisper of a girl, and he had to go six foot four. He doted on that girl, never did see someone so much in love. Not till I met my Delia. Same with your daddy and his daddy, too."

Sandy lowered her head and winked at George, surprising a grunt out of him.

His grandfather sighed long and low before he went on.

"Well, we all knew J.W. shoulda had that conductor job. Put in his time, took care of that train like no one else ever had. But folks further up the line than we was got it in their heads that we had to have that Captain. I figure they was losing money, desperate to keep going somehow. Money drives weak men to make dumb-ass decisions."

George glanced at Sandy, not sure he wanted her to hear the full range of her great-grandfather's vocabulary. She grinned back at him. She didn't have to say a word to remind him she saw and heard worse than that every single day.

George finally managed to relax and lose himself in the story, one he hadn't heard since he was younger than his daughter.

"Young as I was, I knew that particular decision was bad, probably cause trouble," Adam said in a quiet voice. "Never knew it would lead to a dead man, and his woman, and a whole bunch more besides. This here's how it all started."

Chapter 6

1901

Adam Evenschmidt strained with the effort of leaning far enough forward without stepping out of the line of boys waiting to meet the new conductor. At fourteen and smaller than all the others, he was already at a disadvantage. No need to make it worse by setting himself up as a troublemaker on day one.

They all waited in the observation car, easily the fanciest part of the train. The floors were carpeted, the seats upholstered with matching burgundy fabric, and the dark wood and brass fixtures gleamed.

Adam hoped he'd be able to work his way up to the cleaning crew someday. That job was hard, sure, but it had to be easier and less filthy than shoveling coal around and feeding that boiler in the locomotive.

"Adam," a wiry black-haired boy next to him whispered. He was too big and too much older to ignore.

"Yeah, Chris."

"What we standing around here for? Waste of damn time."

"Just the new boss is all, gonna run this whole show now."

A skinny blond boy on the other side, one of the serving crew for the dining car, shook his head.

"Chris got it right. All just for show. Big captain back during the war, but his daddy bought that for him. Doesn't know how to do a damned thing but strut around with his chest stuck out."

"Hold it down, boys," a deep voice said from right behind Adam. "Don't matter how or why, this man's in charge now. Don't be actin' a fool and everything be just fine."

Adam glanced across at the blond boy, the one with all the good information, but he was still shaking his head. None of the boys dared contradict J.W., standing with his hand on Adam's shoulder now.

Everyone working on that train, from the cook to the drivers to the scruffy coal boys, knew J.W. Gartin should have had that top job. No one knew this equipment or the route far up into the mountains better. He'd put in his time and earned the promotion, fair and square.

Not a one of them dared say it, but they all knew why he hadn't gotten it, too.

The whispering and shifting around slowed to Adam's right, and he settled down himself. That had to be the boss. A man stepped into the car, and Adam tried not to frown. He was old, way older than anyone else working on this train. His splotchy pale face was wrinkled under his stiff round hat, and frizzy white hair poked out around the edges.

Adam was sure the hem of the long, gray jacket should have come close to the man's knees, but the belt with a gleaming yellow buckle raked sharply upward over a firm belly. A double row of buttons, the same bright yellow, ran from the collar down to the misplaced waist. A faded red sash crossed the man's chest, and the embroidered swoops around the wrists were discolored and missing in places.

Brand new dark blue pants and shiny black boots made the rest look even more seedy and kind of pitiful.

After a few seconds, Adam finally recognized the hat with the tiny sharp brim. This strange old man was wearing part of his Confederate uniform to go with his railroad uniform. Adam knew from a lot of examples and one experience that he or any of the other boys would be in big, serious trouble if they randomly mixed up their uniforms that way, or if they wore anything so ratty and beat up in the passenger cars.

The owner of the railroad walked right behind the new man, the first time Adam had seen him since he started the job. Mr. Pennebaker's hair was jet black, glistening, and perfectly arranged around a razor-sharp part right down the middle. The flat, rounded hat he carried and his fine black suit were so crisp and fresh it looked like the creases would cut a plain old working boy's skin.

He held up his hand, and everyone went still and silent.

"Ladies and gentlemen, boys and girls, I'd like to introduce to you Captain Jessie Rutherford Akers. He served with honor during the war effort, and we owe him our gratitude. Do your very best to serve him with pride, just as he served us."

The man, captain in a war lost over twenty years before Adam was born, swept through the car without so much as a glance at any of the young workers. Once he and the owner passed into the next car, a general commotion broke out in their wake.

J.W. Gartin stepped into the middle of the train immediately, his huge brown hands held up at shoulder height.

"Hush now. You may feel like you got something to say

right now. Truth is every one of us has a job to do. Damn lucky to have it, too. Go on, now. All of us need to get to work."

That optimism and determination didn't last long, not even coming from one of the rail line's best workers. Adam spent most of his days up in the front of the train, shoveling and loading coal, crawling inside and scrubbing the sooty boiler when it was down, doing the dirtiest jobs that kept the big train rolling.

As long as he kept the fireman, Mr. Hatcher, looking good, Adam got to mostly keep to himself. But he heard bits and pieces of everything from the network of boys all up and down the line.

Turns out Captain Akers picked up right away on who everyone else thought should have his job. J.W. never said a word or showed any kind of reaction, but everyone else saw it. The Captain took to following that good man around, watching everything he did. Before long, problems came up that didn't make any sense if you weren't paying close attention.

Adam paid very close attention.

All of a sudden, after years of taking care of that train like it was his own flesh and blood, things showed up half done or done wrong altogether wherever J.W. went. No one ever caught who did it, or who undid it. No one doubted what was going on, either.

The man himself kept quiet, nodded, and made the repairs. No matter how loud or mean the problems were pointed out.

Adam could see Jessie Rutherford Akers didn't like that, not one bit. If he thought running that train was going to work just like his paid commission in the Confederate Army did, that Captain was disappointed right quick. He wasn't getting the foolish, angry kickback he was looking for. Even after he brought on more men from the Confederacy and they all were in on it together, he drove himself crazy trying to figure out how to goad his target into foolhardy action.

The problems got more serious, and the time and repetition added up. Finally, one day when the train was running empty, heading up the mountain to pick up a load of people, cargo, and mail, the good man had had enough. Neither Adam nor anyone else ever knew if it was the loose coupling that could have caused the whole train to crash or just the never-ending grind of trouble, but J. W. went over the edge.

Chapter 7

2015

MARY SAT UPRIGHT, her breath drawn to finish the scream she'd started in response to the train's hissing steam. She gasped instead, grabbing for the jacket she'd managed to draw over herself.

The air still felt like she was inside a deep freeze rather than late summer, even in the mountains. She no longer heard the train or anything else, and the girl had disappeared with the dream.

She stretched out again, glancing at her watch. Just past six in the morning. No one else would be stirring yet, not after the way they'd worked yesterday. She pulled her sleeping bag up around her shoulders, shaking her head at the frost all over the dark blue fabric. It was thick enough to flake off everywhere except right over her chest.

Where the girl had been.

"Body heat," she said under her breath. She pulled the jacket over herself for good measure. "Nothing but body heat. Mid-fifties overnight my ass."

Even after two cups of scalding hot coffee later that morning, Mary still shivered. No one else seemed to have been affected by the chill, or at least they weren't admitting it. She finally caught Mia right before they started work for the day.

"How are you not freezing right now?" Mary said, trying to keep her teeth from chattering.

"Are you kidding me? It was stifling last night. I would have killed for a ceiling fan." Mia held her hands about a foot apart. "A tiny little tent-sized ceiling fan."

Mary frowned, not sure if Mia was trying to tease her.

"I had frost on my sleeping bag this morning. You're telling me you were hot?"

Mia put the backs of her fingers against Mary's forehead, a confused smile on her face.

"You don't feel sick or anything. Sounds to me like you had one of your famous nightmares, Mar. Maybe you should sleep closer to the rest of us tonight."

Whatever chill had hold of Mary didn't let go until nine that morning. She was so relieved to be warm that she didn't mind the sweat stains on her t-shirt when she finally took the jacket off. Mia kept an eye on Mary all day long, but she didn't mention their conversation until they were getting ready to settle in for the night.

"You okay? Feeling better?"

"I'm fine, Mia," Mary said, and she almost meant it. That dream hadn't left her since she opened her eyes that morning. "Too tired when I went to bed, I guess."

"Well, I still think you should sleep closer in," Mia said. "Being right beside the woods would creep anyone out."

"Don't worry. If something comes in after me, you'll be the first to know."

Chapter 8

1901

ADAM WAS GETTING a drink of water back in the dining car when J.W. went charging through like a roaring bull, not giving a damn who saw him or heard what he had in his mind. The boy's jaw dropped at the foul words boiling out of the man's mouth. Before the grandmotherly black woman who ran the kitchen could grab him, Adam ran forward after J.W.

He was sure he'd be last in line trailing behind, but everyone else was frozen in open-mouthed shock or trying to disappear. Even after Adam passed by, only a handful of the older boys fell in behind him. They all stopped at the coal car.

Even caught up in the relentless need to follow the shouting he heard over the noise of the train, Adam knew he should stop too. Crossing between the cars was hard enough when the train was sitting still. Adam held no illusions about what those massive wheels would do to him if he fell.

Instead he stepped forward, holding onto the door frame

as long as he could. He took a deep breath and pushed himself across the shifting coupling, trying not to look at the huge gravels underneath. The train was moving slowly, gaining altitude on the way up to the mountain resort, but Adam didn't try to fool himself into thinking it would be fine if he slipped off.

Even if he didn't manage to go right under the huge steel wheels, he was quite certain no one would be willing to stop to pick him up. He'd be stuck out here in the middle of nowhere, the most remote part of the line, for at least a couple of days with the temperature below freezing every night.

He leaned forward and grabbed the ladder on the back of the coal car, gripping so hard his knuckles ached. His boss, Mr. Hatcher, must be far enough back in the cars that he hadn't heard what was going on yet. He certainly would have stopped Adam and pinched his ear for him. No lowly fireman's boy should dare pull a stunt like this.

Adam swung himself up the ladder, still holding tight as he could with his sweaty palms. J.W. must have pulled himself up this same way, with much stronger adult hands and his fury to drive him. Once he crouched on top of the sooty roof of the tinder car, Adam tried again to make himself stop, climb back down, and hope no one reported what he'd done so far.

Louder shouts up in the locomotive kept him moving.

He saw J.W.'s large footprints and followed right down the middle. Adam had helped shovel half a load of coal into the tinder car before they'd headed out, same as usual. The train never carried heavy extra fuel up the mountain if they could help it. A full load of coal wouldn't have swayed nearly so much, keeping Adam's heart in his throat with every step he took.

He finally took a breath when he got to the front ladder.

He knelt, grabbing the vertical rails with both hands, intending to climb down to the locomotive. The doors to the cab stood open on either side of the firebox. Gaps in the closed metal fire door glowed red with the engine under climbing stress.

Adam found he could see well enough from where he was.

That Captain, one of his guards, and the engineer were all crowded into the tiny cab with the huge raging man. Adam had barely started learning how the knobs and gauges worked in there, and he was afraid one of them would knock something dangerously out of place. The engineer huddled as far against the right wall as he could without taking his hand off the throttle.

The guard was trying to push J.W. back without much success. That Captain just stared up at the big man, a mean little smile on his face.

Adam held his breath when the black plume of smoke came his way, a habit learned from long hours working around trains. He'd never tried to ride right on top of one in motion. Keeping from breathing in the filthy air, getting it in his teeth and throat and ears, was impossible.

"Don't care what happen no more, gonna put you under the ground!" J.W. shouted.

"By all means, then," Captain Akers said, not nearly as loud but perfectly clear. "Be my guest."

The guard, still struggling to hold the huge man back, glanced at his Captain. At a nod, the guard raised his hands and stepped aside.

From his vantage point on the high roof of the tinder car, Adam could see the metal club held behind the Captain's back.

"No!"

His warning shout, too late, was drowned out by J.W.'s

roar as he darted forward, faster than Adam would have thought he could move. Even quicker, nearly invisible to the boy's eyes, the club swung up and around, hitting J.W. squarely on the temple.

He looked puzzled for a few seconds as blood flowed down the side of his face. The Captain's second blow knocked him out cold.

When Captain Akers stepped aside, J.W.'s seemingly boneless body fell toward the narrow front door. There was a catwalk out there, but it was not as wide as the falling man. The guard jumped to try to catch J.W., but all he got hold of was the man's pants.

J.W.'s upper body slipped over the edge hard enough that the guard was pulled forward. The train jerked then, and Adam nearly fell over the edge of the coal car.

"Help me, goddamn it!" the guard shouted, the strain of holding a man up by his legs clear in his voice.

"Might as well let the garbage take itself overboard," Captain Akers said, but he wedged himself into the tiny space and grabbed the guard around the chest. They both leaned back and pulled. J.W.'s body slowly reappeared inside the cab.

All but one part.

When the engineer saw what had happened, a bloody stump where the good man's head should have been, he screamed high and thin like a little girl. The train jolted again when he let go of the throttle, then pushed it over way too hard.

Adam had never been more grateful he'd missed a meal in his life.

"What the hell we gonna do now?" the guard shouted, backing up until he nearly fell out the door himself.

"This isn't the first dead man we've had to deal with, Hadley," the Captain said, carefully blotting the blood from his uniform with a white handkerchief already stained red.

"In case you ain't noticed, the damn war is over, *Captain* Akers! No one pins medals on a murderer's chest. Gonna slam us both in prison and throw away the keys!"

"And who's going to report any of this?" The Captain tossed the handkerchief out the window as if he didn't have a care in the world, then put his hand on the driver's shoulder. "This good engineer has been so generous with his time, teaching me how to run this locomotive. You would do no such thing, would you Mr. Reynolds? Certainly not a few months before your retirement?"

"No, no, never say a word to nobody," the wiry old man said, staring straight ahead at the beam of bright light illuminating the rails ahead.

He'd always been patient and kind teaching Adam the controls, too, but the boy had a sinking feeling Reynolds was going to keep his promise to the Captain.

"I feel quite sure you'll manage to keep your mouth shut," the Captain went on. "Won't you, Hadley?"

The guard pushed the sweaty red hair out of his eyes, shaking his head.

"Whole damned train saw J.W. come charging up through here," he said. "Think every last one of 'em gonna keep your secret for you?"

"We've been through this before. All we do is clean this mess up so Engineer Reynolds here doesn't have to. Then we deal with whatever happens. Mr. Gartin should have thought before he let himself into the front of the train uninvited."

Adam watched in fascinated horror, unable to move, trying to keep his eyes away from the gory nightmare where J.W.'s head should have been. Captain Akers went through the dead man's pockets, keeping a gold watch for himself and sharing the money between the guard and the engineer. The two men dragged J.W.'s body out to the catwalk again, then tossed him over with grunts louder than the engine.

They mopped up the mess as best they could with spare bits of cloth the fireman used to open and close the firebox, but blood still streaked the floor and out the front door.

Adam realized what was about to happen a second too late. The Captain grabbed a lantern and walked toward the tinder car, no doubt to tap into the engine's water supply to finish the cleanup. Before Adam could move, Captain Akers held up the light.

Adam stared into the man's cold eyes.

"Do I need to tell you what will happen if you ever breathe a word of this, boy?"

"No." Adam forced himself to speak louder. "Nosir. I reckon I know."

"Good," the Captain said, nodding. "I won't stop with you, of course. I'll find every member of your family and send them straight to hell with you and that piece of garbage we just dumped off this fine train. Understand me?"

"Yessir. Understand you just fine."

"Good. Now fetch me down a bucket of water. Then get back there and tell everyone Mr. Gartin jumped overboard." He stopped, shook his head, and smiled. "No, no, you won't say a word. Just as well to let them all work it out for them-selves. Let 'em decide he abandoned the train in the middle of an uphill run, or he never showed up for the return trip. Rumors will take care of the rest like they always do. Damn shame, him so qualified and all."

Adam did as he was told, never suspecting how many decades he had ahead of him for guilt. And regret.

Chapter 9

2015

Mary opened her eyes in the dark, not surprised to hear chattering teeth, to feel violent trembling. The air in her tent was again freezing. She didn't need her light to know the same girl was huddled tight against her.

"Here we are again. My name is Mary Robbins. Can you at least tell me your name? Or what's happening this time?"

"Can't remember my name before I married J.W. Been up here crying for him too long." Mary felt her take a deep breath and hold it for several seconds. She let it out with a whoosh, and spoke for the first time without that terrible fear. "Corrie Belle. Corrie Belle Gartin."

Both women jumped at whistling steam right outside the tent. If this messed up dream with Corrie Belle had set itself to repeat, Mary would meet it head on.

"I'm going to see what's happening out there." The girl clutched tight, but Mary drew back. "You can stay in here. I don't want to keep meeting like this. You must be here for a reason, so let me see what it is."

She slowly pulled the girl's painfully cold arms away and sat up. She held a finger to her lips, then draped her coat over the shivering figure.

"I'll be right back, Corrie Belle. I'm not going further than outside the tent, okay?"

"Devil out there," the girl said, her teeth knocking together. "Killed my husband, kill you too if he get half a chance. Best if you stay put."

"You're probably right. I won't be gone long. I promise."

Mary unzipped the tent door as slowly as she could, though she doubted anyone would hear her over the chuffing, pinging, and rattling noises of the train. She peeked over the top into blinding full daylight.

A huge locomotive sat where the rails would have been a hundred years ago, or close to it. The massive steel wheels floated several inches off the ground. A crowd of well-dressed people, for the turn of the last century, strolled to and from a much smaller observation platform than the one taking shape on the same spot now.

Women wore a dizzying array of bright colored long dresses, their waists cinched tiny and their skirts puffy and full. Mary didn't spot one without a coordinating hat perched on what looked like an unnatural amount of hair. The men wore mostly dark suits, though a few sported pale brown or gray fabric. All of them carried either a porcelain tea cup or a clear cocktail glass.

Several people wearing dark blue uniforms darted through the crowd, refilling beverages or taking away the empty containers. Many of them looked like boys and girls, surely not old enough to be out of school yet.

Mary knew about the derailment that had taken that original deck out along with everyone on the train.

Please, don't be dreaming about that.

She jumped and nearly screamed when an ice-cold hand grabbed hers.

"Make it right," the girl said, still huddled inside the tent. "Make it right. Been waiting so long for someone who could."

"Make what right?" Mary said. "I don't understand what's going on."

"Ain't never found another living soul out here." Corrie Belle huddled beside Mary, tears running down her cheeks. "This place ain't safe for the living, never has been. Not a one of you should be here. Ain't safe for me neither. Don't let me down now, leave me out here forever."

A tall, angry looking man with flaming red hair gave one short blast on a brass whistle, the sliver buttons on his dark blue suit glinting in the sun. The last stragglers got back on board. Their laughter and chatter crashed through Mary's ears.

The girl's grip tightened, but her hand was even colder than before.

"Make it right, Mary. Got to make it right."

Just as the train got rolling, Mary saw movement on the back porch of the caboose. A huge blue sack came hurtling out and landed nearly on top of her tent.

The sack was screaming.

Chapter 10

1901

When the train finally pulled into the depot on top of the mountain late that night, Adam tried to hide his ragged, gnawed fingernails from everyone else. He'd been trying to decide if he should run as fast as he could as soon as the train stopped, or wait back with all the other boys and try to blend in. Maybe if that Captain never laid eyes on him again, he'd forget what the boy looked like.

Adam and several of the other youngest boys usually slept on the train when it was empty. Saved them a dime instead of sleeping in even the cheapest hotel in the resort town. Adam wasn't sure he'd be able to manage to close his eyes anywhere after what he'd seen. He finally decided the best thing would be to walk around all night and see if he could make up his mind about what to do the next day.

He tried to hide in the group of workers heading into town, thankfully walking up the right side of the train where the depot sat instead of the left where J.W. had met his end. Adam hoped to blend in with the wandering crowd of boys, folks who lived in town, and men looking for a little bit of entertainment for the night.

He was so busy keeping his head down that he almost walked right into Captain Akers, waiting at the front of the dining car. Adam thought he would jump out of his skin before he got away, or that the man's eyes would bore a hole right through his skull. The Captain nodded and winked as the boy passed by.

Adam put one numb foot in front of the other, not wanting to draw even a second of attention to himself if he could manage it. The only way he could think of to get through the night, the next day, the next week, was to put the whole thing out of his mind and never think on it anymore.

That worked for about a minute.

Up ahead, just past the depot, a lantern swung low, and a cheerful whistle echoed off the mountainside. That had to be the inspector, coming down to make sure all was well with the train before the crew settled in for the night.

Adam froze, unable to breathe or take even one more step. People passed by him without a word, and he stood alone waiting for the inspector.

"Can't say a word, not to no one," Adam whispered. "Just keep quiet. Not a word."

The inspector didn't break stride or stop whistling as he passed by. He simply nodded and tipped his cap to Adam and kept going. Cold sweat covered the boy's body, and he forced himself to start moving. Put one wooden foot in front of the other, get away from there.

Problem was the inspector was not going along the right side of the train like all the workers just had. He was walking down the left side of the tracks. Adam didn't think they'd managed to wash the blood off the side of the locomotive.

Sometimes they hit animals. Maybe that would be close enough.

Adam had about thirty seconds to believe that.

The inspector passed by the jutting steel cattle catcher on the front, holding his lantern out to get a good look at the wheels and the sides of the boiler. He stopped whistling.

Adam begged and pleaded with his frozen body, desperate to move, terrified of what would happen next.

Before he could get far enough away, the man shrieked.

Adam finally remembered how his legs worked, and he took himself into town as fast as they'd go. Away from that inspector's high wail and everything he knew it meant. He gladly paid the dime for two nights so he could avoid the train altogether.

He never did quite work out how to stay away from the memory, even as an old, old man.

Chapter 11

ADAM WASN'T SURPRISED that a couple of the older boys were happy to make that horrible night worse for everyone who'd missed the excitement. No one seemed to know how it happened that a head was caught in that driving wheel, but those boys knew what it took to get it out.

The fireman had finally used a pickaxe.

The teenagers might have gleefully repeated their story to other employees of the rail line hoping to carry the drama back down the mountain, but it never got that far. Adam didn't know if it was the unspoken rules about keeping to themselves, or if that Captain had threatened everyone. He knew for sure he never did see the same inspector again.

The only boy younger than Adam lasted as long as the return trip back down to Gossdale before he walked away and never came back. The older ones stopped repeating the tale to anyone but themselves before a week went by, but no one who worked on the line ever recovered from that night.

The head was far too chewed up by the wheel, and later by the axe, to identify. But everyone knew J.W. was the dead man. Adam never had to open his mouth to verify or deny that fact.

Everyone also knew the same good man was the cause of problems on the train from that moment on until the end.

Every bit of trouble that Captain or his loyal men ever accused J.W. of causing started really happening. No one ever caught anyone at it, and no one ever admitted to doing it. Still, every single thing that had gone wrong with the train went wrong again, and a bunch of new things besides.

The bigger problem was J.W. had been the only man who knew how to repair all of them. Everyone else put together had a struggle just trying to keep up.

Adam sleepwalked through the days for a couple more weeks, too scared to speak up and too worried about his family starving to death to quit. He watched the train try to take itself apart all around him and did what he could to keep the engine running. He never doubted the reason for all the trouble for an instant.

J.W.'s body never was found out on the line or anywhere else. Even so, Adam was too afraid to look out the window most days, and even more at night. He was too scared he'd see eyes staring back at him, sad eyes wondering why no one ever brought him home or tried to clear his name.

The beginning of the end of the line for Adam came when J.W.'s pretty young wife showed up in that mountain resort town, looking for her husband. He was walking with the other boys, all of them quiet like they had been since that awful night. The girl caught Adam's eye right away.

She was a tiny little thing, dressed head to toe in black with a black lace veil over her face. She stood alone on the walkway beside the depot. Watching.

When the Captain appeared, she walked toward him. Adam and all the other boys huddled around the far side of the building. She barely came up to the man's chest, but she faced him tall and proud as she could. When she lifted the veil, Adam saw her features were so delicate it seemed her agonized expression would shatter her whole face.

"Captain Akers?" she said, her voice high and soft. "I need to know about a man who worked on this train, name of J.W. Gartin? He never did come home."

That Captain stared down at her, as cross as if she'd told him to eat a dog turd.

"Mr. Gartin never showed up the morning after our arrival here a couple of weeks back. Sorry to say no one has seen or heard from him since."

Mrs. Gartin shook her head, then took a step closer.

"I know you had it in for my husband. He told me all the time. That's neither here nor there. I done lost my home over this. Can't weep and moan no more. Please, sir. Please tell me."

This time Captain Akers tilted his head and smiled, but there wasn't a thing friendly about it.

"Well now, *Missus* Gartin, you may want to think on whether he had somewhere else he needed to get to. Or someone else. I have heard tales of things like that. You never can tell, can you?"

That poor girl stood there trembling, tears rolling down her soft, round cheeks, watching that Captain walk away. Watching him strut, more like. Anyone could see he thought he was walking away from trouble and no need to watch behind him.

Adam tried his best to wipe his own tears away before anyone else saw, but he wasn't the only one. This time even the older boys finally seemed to understand.

After everyone else had moved on except Adam, she drew herself up, wiped her face with a fancy black lace kerchief, and walked slow and quiet into town.

Chapter 12

ADAM WASN'T ALONE in noticing one more thing as the days dragged on after J.W. Gartin's murder. Captain Akers must have kept his mouth shut about what happened in the locomotive that night, but he never did hide, trade, or sell the dead man's watch.

Soon as he finished breaking that poor widow girl's heart, that Captain started carrying that timepiece right out in the open. He kept it on the chain stretched across his belly like he had some kind of right to it, and he never bothered to glance around to see who was looking before he checked the time.

The man's own pride brought him down in the end, like such things often do.

Everyone knew Captain Akers didn't own a railman's watch like that. He never had enough time in the job to earn one, certainly not a fine long-working man's model. Adam heard the tales same as everyone else, and he'd seen the truth of where it came from with his own eyes. Word was J.W. got that watch from his own father, a railroad man for years before.

Some of the older boys even whispered how that Captain strangled J.W. with the chain so he could steal the watch for himself. Adam hoped no one believed that one, but he never could be sure.

In that strange way rumors have of overtaking a group of people who spend many long hours together, everyone on that train came to believe that watch was the cause of all the trouble. As long as Captain Akers carried J.W.'s watch, everything was going to fall apart faster than they could fix it. And the only way to make it stop was to get rid of the timepiece.

Adam never could say how it fell to him to stand up to that Captain. He was now the youngest one on the line, and the smallest, and he certainly wasn't known for being courageous. At least not in his own mind.

Not just anyone could go walking up to the front of the locomotive, the reasoning went. On top of that, most of the boys were more than a little nervous that close to a boiler as tall as two grown men. Believing everything on the train was about to fall apart, including that tremendous boiler, didn't help matters.

In the end, Adam admitted to himself that he wanted to be the one. He was still terribly afraid of Captain Akers, but his guilt over what happened to J.W. never stopped eating at his guts. So far down inside that he could pretend it wasn't true, Adam hoped doing this one thing would help some of that burden ease.

His determination didn't help with the fear, certainly not when he was walking toward the front of the train. The air up on top of the mountain was hovering around freezing in the middle of the day by then, but sweat still ran down Adam's back. His feet again felt like two wooden blocks, and his heart pounded so hard he could hear it. But he kept going anyway, toward the Captain standing beside the driving wheel where J.W. lost his life. The man was still wearing his seedy old war uniform even on their off day.

Adam may have been fourteen years old and trembling from head to toe, but that was his first walk as a man.

Mr. Hatcher, Adam's boss, swung down off the coal tinder car, scowl at the ready before he even opened his mouth. With so many things going wrong on a cash-strapped private railroad, not one employee escaped frayed nerves and short tempers.

Adam was walking into a furious knot of men, breaking the new rules about hanging around off-duty and making himself the perfect target for everyone's frustration.

Captain Akers glanced up from his conversation with the new engineer, then turned to see Adam. He walked forward with the same cocky smile he'd had when Adam was frozen on top of that tinder car, too shocked by what he'd seen to get himself away. The boy kept walking, afraid if he paused for even one second he'd run away and never find his courage again as long as he lived.

"Captain Akers, sir," he said, surprised at how strong his voice was. He pulled a far less fine railroad watch out of his pocket, a cheap model provided by one of the older boys. "I was hoping you could tell me the time of day. Want to make sure I set this new watch to match."

For the first time since the Captain strolled through that train, medals shined bright and head held high, Adam saw fear in his eyes. No denying or mistaking it, and no way the man could hide it even if he tried. Adam noticed the gold chain was no longer draped across the uniform, and his heart seemed to stop in his chest. He couldn't tell if it was because of the man, the girl, or the watch itself, but he couldn't pretend the change wasn't real.

The Captain was afraid for his life.

He was right to be.

"I don't have a watch, young man." He looked into Adam's eyes for a second, then turned back toward the locomotive. "Not one you could set yours by."

"I'm sorry, sir." Adam gripped the borrowed watch so hard he was afraid the face would crack. "I thought sure I saw you with a fine gold railman's watch the other day."

"You were mistaken about the quality of that watch, Mr. Evenschmidt," the Captain said, his eyes lighting with anger now. "That was defective, wouldn't keep time worth a damn. Probably a fake. I threw that watch away. Understand me?"

Adam stood for a few seconds, as afraid to look away now as he had been to open his mouth. He didn't yet understand what was happening or why, but he learned right then how a silent battle between two men could turn deadly.

"I understand," he said.

The Captain nodded once, dropped his gaze, and walked away.

Adam saw the fireman move then, probably to order his rebellious charge up into the idle boiler to scrub it. Billy Skeens, the tall boy currently crammed in there as punishment for sleeping during his work shift, would be overjoyed. A cuff on the ear would be preferable to that fate on a freezing cold day.

Rather than face either one, Adam turned on his heel and headed back into town. No one followed him.

He thought that was the end of it, aside from telling the others what he'd heard.

When the train headed back down the mountain, Adam found out how wrong he was.

Chapter 13

2015

Mary's own teeth woke her on the third night, trying to chatter out of her skull. The tent was just as freezing cold as every other time, but she had her sleeping bag to herself. If these crazy dreams had to be so damn frigid, she wished the girl would share what little body heat she had. Or at least tell her why she kept coming back.

She flipped her flashlight on and nearly screamed at the dark shape huddled by her feet. The girl didn't blink or try to cover her eyes when Mary swung the beam that way. She only sat there, bare arms around her bare legs, chin resting on her knees. She stared at the tent wall like she was seeing right through it, expecting the train any second now.

"Here we are again." Mary sat up, clutching the thick fabric under her chin. "Take my jacket. I know you're freezing."

"You think a body ever gets used to being so cold?" the girl said. "Cold way down deep in your bones?"

"I know I don't. Didn't bother me so much when I was your age."

"Never bothered me as a girl." Corrie Belle glanced at Mary for a second, then went back to watching the wall. "Even growing up way down south, didn't feel it. Not 'til I knew what being warm really like. Warm all the way inside your heart."

"You mean with J.W.," Mary said.

She sighed, remembering how shattered she'd been in the days and weeks after losing Rachel. How she'd begged and pleaded with every power she could think of, especially the ones she didn't believe in, to give her just one more second with her wife.

Corrie Belle nodded.

"I never like sleeping without him once we was married. When he stayed up on this mountain. Knew he'd come home to me just as soon as he could, though. That let my heart keep all the rest of me warm. When he never came back, my heart turned dead and cold."

Mary jumped at an airy, low whistle from the valley far below. One long, two short, one long. Miles away from where such a thing could exist, she was hearing a train coming up to a crossing.

Whoever - or whatever - drove that train was sending out a warning.

"That ever happen to you, Mary? Walking around with a dead heart still inside your body? Damn thing just won't stop beating?"

"Yeah, Corrie Belle. A couple of years ago. I lost my love in a car crash. My wife."

The girl looked at Mary again, her delicate, faint eyebrows raised.

"Your *wife*," she said, sounding more curious than upset. "You love her?"

"I loved her more than anything. I still do. I don't know how the hell my heart keeps beating, either. Or why."

Corrie Belle pursed her full lips for a second, then she nodded.

"Tell me her name? I sure would like to know it."

"Her name was Rachel."

Both women turned when the whistle sounded this time, much closer. One long, lonely cry into the darkness.

"Don't think I can do a thing in the world to help your Rachel," Corrie Belle said. "Wish I could, 'cause I hope you can help me."

"What can I possibly do, though? Much as I might want to sometimes, I can't just hide up here in the mountains with you for the rest of my life."

Mary groaned at the harsh tone of her voice, the terrible, angry words. She didn't want to be so hateful to another person, even in a dream.

Especially not to another widow.

"You the only one who can help me," the girl said. She moved forward until she was sitting on her heels, her dark eyes blazing in the flashlight's glare. "May be another hundred years up here alone before anyone sees me. May be never."

Mary reached out, and after a few seconds Corrie Belle took her freezing hand in her colder one.

"Can't you just leave? Float away, or close your eyes and drift away? Maybe if you go somewhere else, you can be at peace."

"No, can't never be at peace." She let go of Mary's hand and shook her head. "Not while my husband's whole life and death nothing but empty space inside of me. Not one trace of him ever found. Could you rest easy if your Rachel up and vanished from the world and you never knew why?"

"I don't know why," Mary said. Her throat ached, but she

was determined not to cry. "I saw where the crash happened, sure, and I saw her body. But I don't know why she left me. Why she was taken from me."

Corrie Belle only stared with those sad, burning eyes.

Mary tried not to, but she couldn't stop herself from trying to imagine it. If she hadn't gotten that heart and soul-stopping phone call in the middle of an ordinary, boring day.

If Rachel just hadn't come home that night, or the next, or the next.

Mary knew she would have spent the rest of her life, long or short, moving heaven and earth to find out what happened. Shivering through a hundred years of cold, lonely nights under these pines would only have been the beginning.

"Tell me what I can do, Corrie Belle. Tell me what I can do."

"Make it right, Mary. Make it right for me, my husband. For you and your wife. None of us can do that ourselves any more. You got to make it *right*."

The whistle screamed from right below camp, louder and moving faster than a bullet train, driving a blast of frigid air through the middle of Mary's frozen heart.

Chapter 14

1901

THE NEXT MORNING, Adam's own name startled him out of his recent habit of walking with his head down, trying to avoid meeting that Captain's eye.

"Evenschmidt! What the hell you going up that way for?"

He turned to see Mr. Wallens, the boss of the freight section. He wasn't a whole lot taller than Adam but he was pure muscle, with a mop of unruly black hair and a thick beard to match.

"I'm the fireman's boy, sir. We got to load water for the trip."

Mr. Wallens shook his head and walked toward Adam, one burly arm held out.

"Guess they never got word to you. You're with me today, probably for a while. Time to learn why all the smart men are at the back of the train, not the front. You're better off back here, anyway. I hear the damn fool owners are thinking about letting that dumbass Captain behind the controls."

Adam opened his mouth, not sure what he had to argue

about. Not the idea of changing jobs, or even a fool like Captain Akers trying to run the locomotive himself. The bright red caboose was just as much the heart of the operation as the locomotive, responsible for critical braking operations and monitoring the whole train for fire or pressure trouble. Working back here was barely a daydream for a lowly fireman's boy.

And truth be told, he'd be thrilled to be that much further away from Captain Akers.

Adam was terribly afraid this was some kind of joke pulled by one of the older boys, maybe even that constant troublemaker Billy Skeens. Just then he saw Billy, trudging along in front of the fireman.

"See you got your new duties, Adam," Mr. Hatcher said, thumping a heavy, sooty hand on Billy's shoulder. "I'll miss you up front. I'm thinking this one might turn out to be no count no matter what kind of beating he gets."

Skeens glared at Adam as they walked on, but Adam was too shocked to respond. He had no idea what had happened, and he didn't care. This was a chance he wouldn't turn down for the whole world.

A couple of hours after they got underway, the dream came crashing down around his shoulders.

Chapter 15

2015

Mary leaned against one of the waist-high stone columns that anchored the new observation deck, the scent of freshly sawn pine boards sharp in her nose. More than enough of the platform had been laid to walk on, and most of the trail crew had already enjoyed the spectacular view of the gorge. Even the safety railing was in place, and Mary had to admit to herself that the thick metal beams were more than sturdy enough for herself and even a hundred others to lean against.

She had no desire to walk out over that vast drop, though, to get closer to the massive boulders so far below. Mary's rational mind knew there was no way she'd see anything left from that crash. She was too high up, and too many years had passed for anything to be left. This trail never would have been approved with such macabre artifacts as part of the gorgeous natural landscape.

But the thought wouldn't leave her mind once it took hold.

What if the clay was extra red because so much life blood

spilled there the day the huge locomotive crashed? What if the white of old fallen trees turned out to be bones baked by a hundred years of sun?

What if the gold watch wasn't the only thing buried in that heavy red Georgia clay? If any of her odd dreams or visions or visitations were actually happening, Mary had seen Corrie Belle thrown from that train right by her tent out in the pines. Unless someone - or something - had taken the girl's remains away, Mary was afraid she remained there still.

Mary turned fast enough to make her own head hurt at a creak of new wood right behind her. Mia held up both hands, trying not to laugh.

"Oh no, I'm sorry! I didn't mean to sneak up on you."

Mary rolled her eyes and tried to smile, then turned back to the gorge.

"I'm a bit jumpy up here, Mia. No worries."

Mia stood beside Mary, leaning her elbows on the thick safety rail.

"Hell of a view. I see why they wanted the trail right here." She turned around, back against the vista, looking into Mary's eyes. "Jumpy is an understatement. What's going on, Mar?"

"Ghosts all around me," Mary whispered before she realized how it sounded. "It's not... Never mind."

She pulled out the watch and held it up by the filthy chain, letting it turn. The gold and glass not coated in stubborn clay flashed in the sunlight. Mia's eyes widened.

"That's a real beauty. Where'd you get it?"

"I found it, back there on the trail a few days ago." She dropped the watch into Mia's cupped hands.

"Looks like it's been up here since the last train ran," Mia said. "Are you going to turn it in? For that museum they were talking about?"

"Yeah, sure. I'll turn it in. That museum is exactly where it's supposed to go."

Mia handed the watch back and stared up at Mary, head tilted to one side.

"You'll turn it in, just not yet."

Mary nodded and smiled. She couldn't get anything past Mia at the best of times.

"You got me, as usual. Not yet."

"Want to tell me why? Talking about it might help."

"It won't help if you think I've finally lost it," Mary said.

"Try me. I've known you for a lot of years, and you haven't scared me off yet."

Mary turned away from the view, facing her green tent huddled alone under the pine trees instead.

"What do you know about that last train?" Mary didn't look at Mia. "The last one that ran up here?"

"Not much. I know it jumped the tracks pretty much where we're standing. After that, they never bothered running another. I think the rail line was losing money anyway."

"No one survived the crash. No one on board, anyway." Now Mary wasn't seeing her tent, the ATVs, or any of the modern world. She saw the colorful long dresses, matching hats for women, dark hats to match their suits for the men. Laughing as they enjoyed their fancy mid-train ride refreshments, while school-aged children waited on them hand and foot. "That's a lot of restless souls, you know?"

Mia glanced over at the campsite. Mary was certain her friend was more worried about her mental state than a fever after a restless night.

"Probably a few ghosts up here roaming around," Mia said. "If you believe in that kind of thing. Are those the ghosts you mean?"

"Maybe. I've been having strange dreams since I found

this watch, Mia. Something I'm supposed to figure out, or change. A puzzle to solve. I think whenever that's done, I can give it to the museum and everything will be right. Right as it can be, anyway."

Mia raised her eyebrows, quick as a flash, but Mary caught it.

"You mean more of your nightmares? Like the ones you have of Rachel?"

"Kind of like those, really. Did I ever tell you what Dr. Rasden told me to do when I woke up? From one of the really bad dreams?"

Mia shook her head. Her brow was drawn down, but she looked more worried than skeptical.

"She told me to engage with them," Mary said. "To talk to whatever was tormenting me, see if I could figure out what it wanted. She said that might get me past my subconscious, past the gatekeeper, down into what I needed to face when I was awake."

"Sounds reasonable to me. Does it work?"

Mary shrugged. "Sometimes. Rachel doesn't really respond or seem to know me, but it works with other people. With the monsters."

"Sounds like the monsters are chasing you all the way up here." Mia rubbed Mary's shoulder. "Think it's because you're on one of these trips for the first time without her?"

Mary took a deep breath, trying not to disagree out of hand. A lost widow girl searching for a savior wasn't all that outrageous compared to the rest of the demons her sleeping mind had conjured. This was one of the few that made sense to her once she opened her eyes.

"Could be. I would have told you I didn't believe in ghosts a week ago, Mia. I'm a lot less sure of that now."

Mia twisted her mouth to one side.

"You know I'm not going to try to dig something out

that you don't want to talk about. And you know you can talk to me about anything you want to. As long as it isn't trying to get you to do something crazy, maybe you're ready to face this particular monster. Think you'll tell me about it someday?"

Mary laughed, nearly surprised into crying. She hadn't realized how afraid she was of Mia thinking she was crazy until that second.

"If it ever makes sense enough to me to tell, I will. I promise."

Chapter 16

1901

Adam stood in the high cupola in the middle of the caboose, staring out over the roof, his jaw dropping at the view of the gorge and the valley below them. His hands ached from holding onto the rail to pull himself up higher and his calf muscles were screaming in protest at standing on tiptoe, but his eyes overrode those crude demands for attention.

It was getting on toward winter, with frost common up on the mountain top. The fire in the little round wood stove bolted to the wall had been a necessity that morning. So much lower, the trees were still putting on a splendid display of red and orange and yellow against the deep blue sky, broken only by dark gray rocks and white water tumbling down out of sight. Adam finally understood why people paid good money to ride this train up and down the mountain, especially this time of year.

Mr. Wallens, Adam's new boss, called up from below.

"Hanging in up here, Adam?"

"Yessir. Everything far as I can see looks just fine."

"Keep an eye on those couplings, now, and watch for smoke from anywhere but that locomotive."

That was the first worry Adam had heard from Mr. Wallens. He was worried himself, then, knowing so many things had been going wrong with the train. This view of the descent to the observation deck was beautiful, sure, but the steep angle was unnerving. The caboose was much higher than the engine with all the cars in between twisted up in the steep S curve.

Adam suddenly didn't want to think about the weight of all those cars on rolling wheels pushing downhill. Just then the brakes sang out, and Adam's lower body felt like it was being pulled forward.

"Long as we watch for hot brakes and bearings from back here, we'll help bring her in safe," Wallens said, clapping Adam's foot.

Adam stayed where he was, doing his best to keep an eye on the train but watching the view more than he should have. He'd never noticed how sharp the right-handed curve coming in to the overlook was, and he did breathe a sigh of relief when the train stopped. Missing that one would send the whole train straight down into that beautiful gorge. By the time he finally climbed down, his hands and feet were full of pins and needles.

"Walk along with us to check the brakes and lines." Wallens stood at the rear exit door leading out onto the metal platform with two other men. "Hardest load they get is coming down that mountain and having to stop. We don't want surprises at the bottom."

That inspection and making sure all the cargo was still in the right place kept Adam busy until the passengers were climbing back on board. He was just about as tired as he'd been loading water and coal by the time he got back to the caboose. He understood now why Mr. Wallens let that little stove's fire go out. Before he could wipe the sweat off his forehead, his whole body ran freezing cold.

Captain Akers stepped inside.

"Just throw it there by the back." He stared into Adam's eyes instead of looking at the man he was talking to.

His flame-haired guard muttered to himself as he stepped past carrying a big blue canvas bag, a lot like the mail bags they normally hauled back and forth. This one landed with a heavier thud than any mail Adam had ever carried. The Captain walked around the caboose as if he'd never been back here before, stopping to riffle through the paperwork on the conductor's desk no one ever saw him use.

Adam managed not to say he probably knew more about how the whole train worked than the old man wearing bits and pieces of his Confederate uniform decades after the war ended. He thought it, though.

"Drag that out to the back porch there, Evenschmidt," Captain Akers said without looking up. "Wouldn't do for the paying passengers to see us throwing out the trash."

Adam didn't want to look weak if he wasn't able to heave the bag onto his shoulder, so he grabbed the end and started dragging. The whole thing shifted and rolled, like it was full of rocks, but he managed to get it against the back rail. He stood out there looking up at the mountainside, the frost line still clear against the pines, hoping that Captain would clear out before Mr. Wallens needed him again.

Just as the whistle blew and the train started rolling, someone spoke right behind Adam.

"Doesn't do to ask too many nosy questions nowadays." Captain Akers moved to stand beside him. "That kind of thing can get a boy into trouble. Or a girl."

The guard squatted down and grabbed one end of the bag while the Captain got the other. On a count of three, they heaved it overboard under the pine trees right at the edge of the clearing, just past the observation deck. It landed in the same weedy patch where Adam had helped dump garbage many times.

None of that garbage had screamed on the way down.

"Another distracting situation cleared up." The Captain brushed his hands together with a loud clap. "Time to get back to things that matter. Right, boy?"

Adam was finally able to turn back once the caboose followed the rest of the train away from the clearing. He tried to convince himself he hadn't seen the bag moving.

The Captain had that same little arrogant smile as the day J.W. died, same as the day he'd strutted away from the good man's grieving young wife.

"Yessir." Adam took a deep breath. "Things that matter."

Chapter 17

1901/2015

THIS DREAMTIME MARY wasn't even in her tent, or in her century as far as she could tell. She stood on a wooden platform that still smelled of fresh pine like that brand new modern observation deck, and all she heard was crickets. The moonlight in the cool air was bright enough to let her see an old-fashioned train depot with deep eaves and graceful curved roof supports, but she couldn't read the name of the town on the sign.

Mary gasped when she tried to breathe in the mixed scents of roasting meat from somewhere close by and sulfurous coal smoke from closer by. Her ribs were in some kind of vise that stretched around to her back and hips. Her waist felt tiny to her hands, and her breasts looked unreasonably large in the dim light. For a few seconds, she thought it was the cut of the long wool skirt she wore that created the illusion. The waist went on forever, covering most of her ribs, and her puffy white blouse billowed out in front and along her arms.

Another attempt at a deep breath convinced her she was wearing a corset, and a vicious one at that. Mary felt a broad hat balancing on her head before she reached up. Her hair was much longer, crudely straightened and twisted into elaborate loops and swirls nearly as wide as the hat.

Not for the first time in a dream, she wished for a camera, or at least a mirror. Even she wouldn't believe this getup when she opened her eyes back in that trailside tent.

Mary heard low voices coming from the tracks where a huge steam train sat. Her ears caught the ticking and groaning of the massive boiler cooling down, and she backed up into the shadows. Several boys came walking toward her. She wondered what they were doing out so late at night by themselves until she got a good look at them.

They might be school-aged, but they were wearing grubby railroad uniforms. They didn't walk with a teenager's springy step, either. These boys moved like middle-aged men just off a long, difficult shift.

Corrie Belle was nowhere to be found.

"Where the hell am I now?" Mary said under her breath after they passed by.

She'd never dreamed of something so far in the past or so vivid. The terrified girl might have come from a time like this, but she still showed up in Mary's modern tent. She was just about to follow the boys and try to find out when she heard more soft footfalls.

A lone boy was walking toward her, shuffling along by himself. This one was smaller than the others, and painfully thin. His clothes floated around his slight frame. He trudged with his head down, and the set of his shoulders brought tears to Mary's eyes.

She didn't care what the time or the situation was. A little boy shouldn't walk like that.

This time a distant whistle from behind her kept Mary

from stepping out into the moonlight when he was right in front of her. She saw a light back that way, moving at about waist high as if a grown man swinging a lantern approached.

The boy froze. He was whispering, almost chanting to himself.

"Can't say a word, not to no one. Just keep quiet, don't say a word."

Corrie Belle's voice echoed in Mary's head, telling her to make it right, make it right. This child was terrified of something, or someone, and she knew with the certainty of a dream that he was about to let his chance pass him by.

She knew just as clearly that this whole business of the girl, the dreams, the watch, all of it turned on what she decided to do right now.

She stepped up beside the boy.

"Shhhh, I'm not going to hurt you," she said when he jumped. "What's your name?"

"Name of Adam Evenschmidt." His words were musical and lilting though his voice was weary. "Sorry, ma'am, no train again tonight."

"No, I don't think I need one. Do you need to talk to that man?"

Adam drew away with a gasp. Mary was afraid he was going to run back the way he'd come.

"Can't talk to him, no ma'am," he said, his thin voice trembling. "Can't talk to no one."

"Not even if I go with you? I'll make sure no one hurts you, Adam."

"Can't stop the devil, ma'am. That Captain the devil. All we do is stay out the way."

Mary glanced toward the whistling. The man looked like an inspector of some kind, and he was nearly upon them. The dreamtime was speeding up, running away from her.

No matter how many nightmares she lived through, aware or not, she always struggled to fight down the panic.

"What if that man coming could call the police, Adam? What if he brought help? Then the devil couldn't get you."

Adam shook his head, his small mouth and eyes scrunched up.

"That Captain, he already said he won't just *get* me. Gonna kill me. Kill me, kill my sisters, then kill my mama. That devil already murdered one good man tonight. He'll kill more and be happy about it."

Mary closed her eyes for a second, trying to force her mind to remember the name. The girl had said that very same thing, her husband was a good man that the devil murdered.

Every man's name she'd ever heard crowded forward, demanding to spring from her lips and be no help whatsoever.

The swinging lamp was only a few feet away.

She tried to keep her desperate cry inside her mind.

Help me, Corrie Belle! Help me save this one child from the devil!

"We can tell him what happened to J.W.," she said, drawing in her breath as the girl's icy fingers caressed her spine. "And then I'll take you out of here, Adam. You've been here long enough. J.W.'s murder won't stay a mystery forever if you help me now. I know this was his, and I'm going to make sure everyone else knows it, too."

Mary held out the watch, shining like brand new instead of scuffed and filthy from a hundred years in the dirt. The boy's huge eyes widened even more, the irises so blue she could see them even in the faint light. He reached out, and she took his pitifully thin hand.

"Stay right here by my side?" He squeezed harder than Mary thought he could. "Don't let go, no matter what?"

"No matter what," Mary said, squeezing back. She turned to face the inspector, right beside them now.

"Excuse me, sir? This boy needs to talk to you. A man was killed on this train tonight." Mary looked down at Adam and nodded. "A man was murdered."

Chapter 18

1985

"Mɪɴᴅ ꜰᴇᴛᴄʜɪɴɢ me a little more water, George?"

George Evans jumped, startled to realize he was in his grandfather's crowded and overly warm bedroom. His back was stiff as a board from sitting there so long, and he caught Sandy rotating her shoulders. His daughter was also trying to wipe tears from her face without anyone seeing.

"I'll go get it, Greatgrand," she said. "If you promise you'll tell the end."

Adam Evans held out his hand, and Sandy took it.

"After carrying this mess round in my head for near eighty years, you best believe I'm gonna finish. Never have told anyone the whole story before now. Bout time I got it out into the open where I can keep an eye on thangs."

Both men watched her walk out of the room with no evidence of her usual bounce. Adam sighed, then turned to George.

"Told her way too much. Shoulda kept my fool mouth shut."

"No, I don't think so at all, Granddad. She's a smart kid. She's just thinking it all over. I am too. Sounds like you left a bunch out every time you told it all those years ago."

"Guess I should lighten up a bit for the rest."

George laughed, hoping Sandy couldn't hear him. No, his granddad had never raised a daughter, much less one so sharp and quick.

"Take it from me on this one." He leaned over to pat the old man's shoulder. "If you do that, she'll never forgive you. Sandy can spot a fake or a liar about a thousand miles away."

"That's a gift that will serve her well," Adam said, rubbing his stubbly chin and nodding. "I'll be just as true as I can, then."

Sandy walked in carrying two glasses and holding a third against her ribs. She examined the recorder for a second, then settled in at her great-grandfather's feet again.

"Okay, tell the rest, Greatgrand. And tell the truth."

Adam winked at George, took a long drink of the water, and leaned back into his tale again.

"That was my last trip on that line, same as it was for a whole lot of folks. Difference was once we made it to Gossdale, I got off, walked away, and kept walking. Never even said fare-thee-well to them other boys. I went into town, found work at a restaurant, and saved up enough to get myself to Atlanta. Got a job on a real train line, and I stayed right there till I retired fifty years later on.

"That train, the one I walked away from into my own life, she only had one more trip left in her. Never did make it back to Gossdale down at the valley end of the line. They headed out after a couple of days, made the trip up okay far as I know. Coming back down was a different story. That's the one so many folks heard of."

"The train crashed in the gorge, right?" George said.

"That's right, George. It's just like they say far as where it all happened. Anyone driving that train knew they had to be certain them brakes worked long before they got to that overlook. Like I said, that was in a big, long curve, and the engineer had to slow her way down before she got there. There's a stretch not long before that last hill goes down where they'd test the brakes, once, twice, three times to make sure they caught good.

"What I heard was they finally let Captain Akers behind the controls, with the train full as it ever was of people and goods and mail. Full load ain't no time to test a green engineer. Course no one knows for sure. No one on the train that day lived to tell me or anyone else the tale. But if that Captain didn't test the brakes going into that bad curve, he got what was coming to him. Well, he got that either way. Most of the ones working that day and none of the ones riding deserved a thing but to get off that mountain safe and sound. Not a lone one of 'em did.

"All anyone knows is that train went sailing off the edge of the gorge, right through the big platform they used to stand on and drink their tea and whiskey. Full train running full ahead jumped right over them tracks and kept going 'til something stopped it. That drop was near nine hundred feet onto solid bedrock. Not even that devil Captain could survive, least not still in his body."

He shook his head, mouth pursed.

"I never did shed a tear for him nor his buddies, the ones that ran that whole train line into the ground. Whole company folded up after that. I'm not too proud to admit I shed plenty for the boys I worked with, those passengers who never had a thing to do with any of that mess, and for that good man and his widow. None of them deserved what happened to them. All I ever could do was hope it was quick and easy for them.

"Course the reason folks tell this tale to begin with is it

don't seem any of them been resting easy. I heard them same stories, ghost train going up and down the line that ain't had tracks for more than sixty years. Folks on both ends hear the whistles and moans, valley and mountain. No reason why such sounds would be there. Only that reason you don't want to believe that I see in your eyes."

Sandy opened her mouth to protest, her cheeks flaming red, but her great-grandfather smiled and held up one gnarled hand.

"Might want to look into it a touch before you decide Greatgrand is talking crazy. You'll find people seem to get hurt all along through there. No good reason for that, neither. That's why them narrow gauge rails are still there in places. Everyone who went up through there after the steel seemed to come to a bad end, only hurt if they was lucky. More than should have ended up dead.

"You can say all you want about things happening just by some kind of coincidence. I heard that before, too. All I know is I wouldn't go up through there myself even if I still could. If I had my way, no one would ever go up through there again. More than enough blood's been spilled. Don't know how it could ever be cleaned up and made right. Whatever ghosts linger up there are still hungry. You best believe that if not one other thing I told you."

George watched Sandy watching her great-grandfather, sure he could see the gears turning inside her head. She'd be wondering right about now whether the old man could be trusted, if he was just pulling her leg or playing a prank.

Sandy had never taken well to those kinds of games, not even when she was a tiny child. The truth was treasured above just about everything else in her life. George knew he was damn lucky to have a teenaged daughter with that as a focus.

"Can we go to the towns?" she said, still looking at her grandfather. "At the ends of the lines?"

"I suppose you two young folks could. Not sure I'm up for the trip, ghosts or no. Sitting in a car for hours ain't the best thing in the world for my old back."

"You think it's safe, though?" she said, twisting her fingers in her ponytail again.

George raised his eyebrows before he could stop himself. He never expected his sensible daughter to believe such a fanciful tall tale, never in a million years. She wasn't putting on, either, trying to be nice and pretend. That nervous twitch with her hair and her wide eyes gave her away.

"I reckon it's safe enough in town." Adam took a long drink of his water. "If you go out there when the wind's right, you might hear that old whistle blowing. Just promise me you won't go near the rails, whatever's left of them. Hardly any narrow-gauge trains left, so those towns may have dried up and blowed away by now."

"Grandad has a couple of doctor appointments on Monday," George said when Sandy turned his way with the question all over her face. "Your mother will be here on Saturday, so maybe you two can run up there then."

"Now if you want to go up to the mountains with your family, you need to go on, George," Adam said, his wrinkled mouth drawing down. "My nurse gets me to my appointments just fine when you or your daddy ain't around, you know."

"Yeah, I know, Grandad. But I think Sandy's the natural born investigator in the family. She'll be just fine without me slowing her down."

"Well, I talked enough for one day, but I got to say one thing more." The old man looked into George's eyes for a long moment, then into Sandy's. "You want to look into this or anything else, Sandy girl, you need to do just that. Don't get into the habit of regret. Not now, not ever. Don't live your life feeling like some part of your heart is frozen, too ashamed and afraid to do what's right.

"I carried that shame of not doing any more than I did for eighty long years, but it don't take near that long to break your heart. You promise me that one thing, both of you, and I'll rest a hell of a lot easier tonight."

George didn't bother wiping his tears away, and he noticed Sandy didn't either.

"I promise, Greatgrand. I promise."

Chapter 19

2015

MARY OPENED the door of what looked like every other house in the tiny little town of Gossdale. Wood-frame, freshly painted, lawn perfectly kept with cheerful white and orange daffodils lining the sidewalk and huge pale yellow, deep pink, and brilliant red azalea bushes against the house. The rhododendrons higher up on the trail hadn't even budded yet.

The interior of the museum was nothing like any of the other modest brick or wood frame houses, at least she hoped so. Shelves and long glass-covered display cases filled all the rooms she could see, and almost every space was full of things somehow related to the railroad.

She clutched the watch, more precious than she ever could have imagined, as she walked around the crowded space. The walls were painted a muted cream, so all of the photos in their dark frames stood out. Mary didn't have to examine many of the images before she knew she was looking at an image of the devil, the man driving that train down into hell. She read the photo caption under her breath.

"Confederate Captain Jessie Rutherford Akers, later conductor of the ill-fated Engine 429 on its last run."

Chills raced over Mary's flesh as she looked into the murderer's eyes, the one who'd killed so many either by his own hand or by his own arrogance. He wore an odd combination of standard dark blue clothing and bits and pieces of his Civil War uniform, faded and threadbare. The medals were carefully pinned on his long jacket, and the stiff, round Captain's hat sat firmly over his gray hair. He held his head high and a little to the right, somehow managing to look sideways and down his nose at the same time.

"Well, Captain," Mary whispered, rubbing her thumb over the cool face of the watch. "I hope we can get a few of your ghosts laid to rest."

Mary jumped when a woman spoke from right beside her.

"Can I help you with something, ma'am?"

She opened her mouth to say no, then paused. The woman was wearing a dark green town logo golf shirt and a blue volunteer badge just like everyone else showing the tourists around, but Mary was sure she'd seen her somewhere before. She was tall and slender, with long reddish-brown hair and bright blue eyes. Mary guessed she was around her own age, but she didn't look it.

She still couldn't imagine why she thought she knew a strange woman in a tiny north Georgia town. Recent events had left her a lot less skeptical than she might have once been.

"Do I… I'm sorry if this sounds strange, but have I seen you somewhere?"

"That's not strange, no," the woman said, her pale cheeks flushing a little. "I get that a lot. I'm Sandy Evans, an investigative reporter with CNN down in Atlanta. I volunteer up here when I get the chance. My grandfather worked for the railroad."

Evans. An echo of Adam Evenschmidt, the little boy from her dream. Mary grunted and shook her head. She wasn't about to go down that road, not without a much better reason.

"That's it, I've seen you on the news. I'm Mary Robbins. You probably can help me." She hoped the words would come if she just started talking. "I don't know if you've heard about the new bike trail here? Anyway, I've been working out there all week, and I found something. I thought you might like to have it for the museum."

When the watch left her hands, what Mary could only explain as hot chills raced over her body before she felt a profound calm. Sandy turned the watch over, then looked up.

"Oh yeah, we know all about the trail," she said, smiling. "Helped us get a few much-needed grants to spruce this place up a bit. Any idea where this watch came from? It looks too old for our rail line here."

"Well, that's where it gets a little strange," Mary said, her own face turning red. "The story I was told is it belonged to a man who worked for another line, but a man named J.W. Gartin carried it later. He worked on the route going up the mountain. Lived here in Gossdale, too."

Sandy's jaw dropped, and she blinked slowly.

"Did you say Gartin?"

"Yeah. You've heard that name before?"

"Let's just say he was the basis for my entire career." Sandy shook her head. "Assuming you're not protecting a source, want to tell me who told you this?"

Mary took a deep breath, chewing on her lower lip. Sandy didn't seem like the sort who'd try to play games or catch her in some kind of trap. She didn't want to give everything away all at once, either. Might as well go with a different name from her nighttime adventures, the one she'd been afraid to try earlier.

"Does the name Adam Evenschmidt sound familiar?" Mary tried not to hold her breath.

Sandy drew back with a faint breath of laughter. Mary's fears of sounding like an idiot disappeared when she saw tears in the other woman's huge blue eyes.

Just like that little boy's eyes in the moonlight in her dream.

"I'd say more than familiar," Sandy said, her chin trembling. "Adam was my great-grandfather's name, and he was born Evenschmidt. He changed it during World War I like a lot of folks with German names did. Adam worked on the train going out of Gossdale, just like J.W. Gartin. The rail line you've been turning into a trail. I've never believed in coincidences, Mary. Certainly not one as big as this. Want to tell me how you knew the name he changed a hundred years ago?"

"Not really," Mary said. The laughter bubbling in her chest felt like a locomotive with way too much steam built up. "But it's only fair. I dreamed about him a couple of nights ago. Right up there on that trail."

Sandy mouthed *wow* to herself, but she was smiling.

"You found my Greatgrand's ghosts. In a hurry? I've got something you need to see."

Chapter 20

THE TWO WOMEN walked through to the back of the museum, past more photos and huge glass cases full of everything from railroad lanterns and ancient coins to what looked like rusty old camping gear. Sandy stopped beside the only closed door in the house and pulled an overloaded key ring out of her jeans pocket.

"This is the archives room," she said. "Hardly anyone knows it's here, and the ones who do are quite careful and serious, but we still lock it. Thankfully one of the donations we got a while back was an old videotape recorder, kind of a special one. It transferred Betamax to VHS."

They walked into a room full of shelves like the others, but these were filled with containers of every size imaginable. Huge, cardboard document boxes covered the carpeted floor under the bottom shelf, and everything from videocassettes to DVDs to tiny USB drives lined the shelves. A huge flat panel TV covered one wall.

Once her mind stopped spinning and caught up to the odd word the woman had used, one she hadn't heard in decades, Mary laughed out loud before she could stop herself.

"Did you say Betamax? I don't think I've heard that since the Eighties."

"Exactly." Sandy grinned. "That's when I got my start. I guessed wrong on which format would win out on the consumer side, but I recovered fast. Have a seat, this will take me a minute."

Mary sank into one of the burgundy-upholstered office chairs, thankful for the thick cushioning under her sit bones. She'd had just about enough of roughing it, at least for another year. Sandy pulled a DVD with a hand-written label from one of the top shelves and leaned over to turn on the TV and a player.

"Getting these off of Betamax was a start, but VHS degrades quickly. Soon as I could, I transferred all my old tapes to DVD. I'll eventually get around to Blu-ray or what-ever the standard is by then." She sat down beside Mary and grabbed a remote from the middle of the oval wooden table, leaving nothing but a box of tissues, a digital recorder, and a plain spiral notebook in the space. "Please excuse my hideous hair and clothes. It was my first official interview."

Mary wrinkled her nose. "No worries. Don't even get me started on the sins of toxic chemicals and flammable Eighties hair."

Mary couldn't hide her sympathetic smile when a much younger version of the lovely woman beside her appeared on the screen. Her eyes and hair color were recognizable, but the towering teased bangs and bouncy side ponytail were cringe-inducing. A green and purple plaid button-up shirt with huge matching plastic earrings completed the regrettable ensemble.

"I'm apparently the reason they invented stylists," Sandy said, her face now bright red.

"You're not alone. My high school yearbooks are in a locked vault."

The teenager introduced herself as a reporter on the ground in Decatur, Georgia, with a confidence and ease Mary could see even thirty years in the past on a grainy video. Sandy promised the best ghost story the viewers would ever hear, told by her great-grandfather who lived through the whole thing.

A painfully cheesy wavy dissolve cut switched to another video showing a very old man with the same big blue eyes as Sandy. The same as that terrified little boy from her dream. Before Mary could say anything about that, he started telling his story.

It wasn't just any story, a random recollection of life in a harder, simpler time. His words were the flesh and bones to the ghosts who'd been tormenting Mary the whole time up on that mountain. All the missing parts of the girl's tales and confusing questions fell into place like a mirror breaking in reverse.

Mary's tension and worry and certainty that she was losing her mind drained away minute by minute, like pressure venting from an overheated boiler. By the time the teenaged girl came back on with her utterly charming wrap-up of her very first paranormal investigation, tears were running down Mary's cheeks.

The little boy who was too terrified to report that horrible crime brought it to life when he was an old, old man.

Sandy didn't say a word, showing one of her best skills as an adult investigator. She simply held out the box of tissues.

"It's the same story. Everything matches up. Even the parts I didn't know."

"What does it match up with, Mary?"

"I can't think of any way to tell you without sounding as

crazy as I've been feeling," she said, wiping her eyes once again.

"Well, let me tell you a secret even bigger than my great-grandfather's birth name." Sandy kicked off her shoes and tucked her legs up on the chair underneath her. The professional reporter had obviously left the room. "That day, I believed every word Greatgrand said. Even when my mother brought me up here a week later, when she and my father helped me with the research and we kept coming up empty, I believed him. Some part of me always has. I have a strong hunch what you're about to tell me is what I've been searching for all these years."

Mary stared at the woman in front of her, now looking far more like that enthusiastic teenager than the serious, determined professional who didn't flinch away from horrible criminals, powerful world leaders, or renowned experts in any field.

Maybe this was what the ghost girl meant by making it right, more than helping the boy in the dream. As simple as making sure someone knew what really happened. That was what Corrie Belle wanted badly enough to huddle alone and freezing by that extinct railroad track for more than a century.

If nothing else, verifying J.W.'s side of things, bringing him back from the long lost dead, might be what it took to get Mary's own nightmares to stop.

Mary started talking, going back to the first glint of that watch in the heavy red clay, and Sandy never moved. She listened intently, and Mary was sure the notepad, recorder, or camera were there during Sandy's professional interviews just to make things easier for other people.

She had no doubt that Sandy took in and remembered every detail.

"I know exactly how it sounds." Mary drew a full breath

into her lungs for what felt like the first time in days. "Honestly, I'd vowed to never mention any of this to another living soul and hope to never see another dead one to tell. I'm glad I told you, though."

Sandy closed her eyes, shaking her head for a few seconds.

"That answers more questions than I ever thought to ask. I'll tell you what I want to do, and I hope you'll be willing to help. I've had a few people bugging me for years to upload some of my old interviews, but I've never done it. Not just embarrassing, but most of them were too damn silly."

"Are you thinking of putting this online?"

"No, not quite." Sandy blotted at her eyes. She held up the watch again, letting it swing gently from the chain Mary had tried her best to clean. "I'd like to see this in a display by itself with a monitor showing my investigative debut right above it. I was able to dig up a little information about that Captain before he met his end, and a bit about the Gartins. If we include some of that to finally tell their story, that will fulfill a whole bunch of wishes all at once."

"Eighties hair and all?" Mary said, too overwhelmed with the idea to think of anything else.

"Sadly, yes to the hair. And I can't believe I'm saying this, but maybe not just in the museum. Those grants I mentioned earlier? We could probably get a hell of a lot more if I do a TV piece about the trail opening after years of rumors. Gossdale is a lovely little town, but it's about to dry up and blow away. Keeping a story like this hidden misses one of the smartest ways to bring people up here. Even if we have to put up with ghost hunters descending on us, we could really turn that around."

"I can't imagine you believe this enough to put it out there even in the museum, much less on TV."

Sandy snorted.

"If I'm going to admit I got my start as a teenaged paranormal investigator, everything will be downhill from there. It's the least we can do for these folks, especially after they answered thirty years of questions. As for believing you, I told you why I do."

"More like a hundred years of questions for one of them," Mary said. "Did you ever find a picture of her? The girl?"

Sandy grinned and got to her feet in one graceful motion.

"Great idea!"

She walked to one of the shelves without a word, leaving Mary wondering what great idea she possibly could have had without realizing it. After rustling through one of the smaller boxes, Sandy sat down with something held under the table.

"I don't need reassuring, but you hit upon the best way to settle yourself down." She put three black and white photos of young African-American women on the table. "Now, which one's your ghost? Greatgrand never knew her name. I found it later on. I'd bet she told you, though."

Mary wondered if she should make a show of trying to figure it out or just point to the one she'd recognized instantly. She'd spent too much time with that terrified face to ever have a doubt. She decided to be as direct as Sandy was and pointed to the one on the left.

"Corrie Belle Gartin."

Sandy turned the photo over. Neither woman was surprised to see the name printed on the back.

"I guess it was a pretty good idea after all," Mary said. "What can I do to help?"

Chapter 21

THE OBSERVATION DECK, the gorge, and the whole mountain range looked different to Mary's eyes a few short weeks later. Green metal plaques with white lettering pointing out mountain and waterfall names were interspersed with historic information about the river, the railroad, and the towns at either end. The trees were lush and dark green, the rhododendrons in the undergrowth covered in clusters of dark pink, purple, and white flowers.

A few curious cyclists stopped to take in the view, then stayed to watch the unexpected event of a small television crew setting up. Mary had ridden up from Gossdale with Sandy Evans and her camera and sound people. Even with trail work soreness behind her, she was happy to walk the quarter mile from the new parking lot rather than chug up the mountain on a bike.

The camera was tiny compared to the massive Betamax recorder now on display in the museum back in Gossdale. Mary knew the video quality would be far superior, though, especially with the small tubular microphone Sandy tucked under the collar of her light jacket. The breeze was much warmer than during the trail work trip, but chilly compared to Atlanta, already stifling in mid-June.

Finished with her technical preparations, Sandy joined Mary on the observation deck.

"It's gorgeous out here," she said. "Greatgrand never forgot that, no matter how upsetting most of his memories were. Ready for your big debut?"

Mary's stomach did a slow, twisting roll.

"Are you sure that's a good idea? I don't want to ruin your whole segment when I forget how to speak English."

"Well, it wouldn't be the first time," Sandy said with a crooked smile. "You'll do great. All you have to do is talk about building the trail, point out where you found the watch. You okay with talking about dreaming the names?"

"Why stop now?" Mary touched the watch, safely in the front pocket of her blue jeans instead of tough old trail work pants. "Sure this isn't going to cause you trouble?"

Sandy laughed, the light, free sound of it more reassuring than words.

"We won't get into the sensational stuff, don't worry. I'm just going to tie the trail work to getting the watch into the museum. If you're not happy with how you do for some reason, we have plenty of time for more than one take."

"Let's go before I lose my nerve."

Mary stood off to the side, watching Sandy walk slowly along the observation deck. She had no notes, but she described what was behind her perfectly. The young woman with the camera followed, making sure to keep the stunning views in frame the entire time. Sandy turned to Mary, held out her arm, and smiled.

Mary stayed calm enough through the questions, managing to speak slowly instead of keeping pace with her pounding heart. She was fine until Sandy asked about the watch, the thing that brought the two of them together.

She clutched the cold metal with a rigid grip, somehow certain she'd drop it over the edge and lose it forever.

"You're doing great," Sandy said, beaming. "Don't worry, we'll edit this bit out. Adam would be so proud of you."

Mary twisted the chain through her fingers and slowly pulled the watch out. The flash of the bright sun against the newly cleaned glass face blinded her for a few seconds, but she kept talking.

When she blinked several times and looked back toward the crowd of bikers behind the camerawoman, Mary was thankful Sandy had taken over the interview again.

Faint like the afterimage of that sun glare, she saw a much bigger crowd. Instead of everyone wearing black bike shorts and multicolored tight-fitting shirts, the men wore dark suits with high starched white collars. The women wore long bright dresses. Some of them carried small umbrellas, and most had their hair piled on top of their heads or hidden under massive, broad hats that matched the gowns.

Mary caught the drifting scent of coal smoke, heard the chuff of the steam locomotive.

When Sandy wrapped up the interview, the small crowd broke into spontaneous applause. The noise Mary heard went far beyond a handful of cyclists. Easily a hundred spectral train passengers clapped, many of them cheering.

A grinning young boy stood close to the front, his eyes as big and blue as the woman beside Mary. A huge black man in the dark blue uniform of the railroad held a tiny woman in a pale pink gown close, both of them seeing only each other.

And the most gorgeous woman, her face and form known through not enough years and countless dreams, stood right in the middle. Rachel was as beautiful as on their wedding day, though she wore her favorite trail work purple shirt and green pants instead of a flowing white gown.

She held her left hand over her heart, the ring flashing as bright as the old railman's watch.

Mary heard her beloved's whisper, somehow cutting through the noise.

"You made it right, Sweetheart. For all of us."

ABOUT KARI

Kari Kilgore's wanderlust and imagination lead her all over the world on grand adventures. Her heart and family bring her home to her native Appalachian Mountains of Virginia. From that solid base, she and her husband Jason A. Adams bring those adventures to life in fiction.

Kari writes science fiction, fantasy, horror, and contemporary fiction, and she's happiest when she surprises herself. She lives at the end of a long dirt road in the middle of the woods with Jason, various house critters, and wildlife they're better off not knowing more about.

The Confidential Adventure Club

For Kari's exclusive free After The End stories and deleted scenes, discounts, early pre-sale releases, adorable pet photos, and a whole lot more not available anywhere else, visit The Confidential Adventure Club at www.smarturl.it/c-a-club.

Hope to see you there!

www.karikilgore.com
www.spiralpublishing.net

ALSO BY KARI KILGORE

I hope you enjoyed reading *In the Pines* as much as I enjoyed writing it. Check out more of my fiction at www.karikilgore.com.

The Confidential Adventure Club

Want more fiction from Kari, including stories, discounts, and box sets not available anywhere else? Want to hear about locations, research, and other cool things that inspired this story and beyond? All that and adorable pet photos, too?

Join The Confidential Adventure Club and get a thank you gift of a free short story and a whole lot more at www.smarturl.it/c-a-club.

Hope to see you there!

Novels:

Until Death

The Dream Thief

Dreaming the Storm: Book One of the Storms of Future Past Series

Joining the Storm: Book Two of the Storms of Future Past Series

Fighting the Storm: Book Four of the Storms of Future Past Series

Novellas:

Songs in the Mountain

Legacy of the Land

Restricted Species

The Becalmed

Into the Storm: Book Three of the Storms of Future Past Series

Short Stories:

Renovations

Intentions

The Garbage Belt

The Seeds of Love

Wicked Bone

The Sound of Murder

Terminalia

Little Five: A Terminalia Story

Reflections

Collections:

Fantastic Women: A Dark Fantasy Novella Trio

Fantastic Shorts: Volume 1 - A Fantasy Short Story Collection

> "Kari Kilgore is an author to watch—her lyrical voice a siren song; her insight, conjured voodoo."
>
> —Richard Thomas, author of *Breaker* and *Tribulations*